Esther
The
Easter Donkey

Written by Nora Ballew
Illustrated by Matt Zeigler

The Legend of the Jerusalem Donkey

The story told of the Jerusalem or 'Easter' Donkey is that this particular type of miniature donkey had been Jesus' mount on Palm Sunday when He first rode into the city of Jerusalem.

Jesus chose to ride a donkey because it was the humblest of all the beasts of burden, and it had been prophesied that he would arrive on the back of a donkey.

"Now when they drew near to Jerusalem and came to Bethphage, to the Mount of Olives, then Jesus sent two disciples, saying to them, "Go into the village in front of you, and immediately you will find a donkey, and a colt with her. Untie them and bring them to me. If anyone says anything to you, you shall say, 'The Lord needs them,' and he will send them at once." This took place to fulfill what was spoken by the prophet, saying, "Say to the daughter of Zion, 'Behold, your king is coming to you, humble, and mounted on a donkey, and on a colt, the foal of a beast of burden.'" Matthew 21:1-11 ESV

When the time came that Jesus was to be killed by hanging on a wooden cross, Jesus' gentle donkey followed and watched as Jesus was forced to carry his heavy cross up the hill of Calvary. Seeing this tragic event taking place, the young donkey wished with all her heart that she had been able to carry the cross for Jesus, as she was the proper one to carry heavy burdens. She was called a 'beast of burden' after all.

Deeply saddened by what was happening to her master, the donkey turned her back on the sight, but she would not leave. She wished to stay until the end, because of her love for Jesus.

As a reward for the loyal and humble love of the little donkey, the Lord cast the shadow of the cross to fall across her back. He left it there for generations of the Jerusalem donkey to carry forever as a sign that Jesus carries our burdens and the love of God carries a reward for us all.

It was spring time at Potter's farm. Yellow Daffodil flowers grew beside the big red barn and the fruit trees were heavy with fresh new buds. Three baby chicks had hatched from their eggs and chirped *"peep-peep-peep"* as they followed Mama Hen around the barnyard. Papa Rooster was proud and crowed, *"Cock-a-doodle-doo!"*

Also living in the barnyard, were two lady pigs. They were sisters named Maisy and Daisy. They were pudgy old pigs who loved to play in mud puddles. They giggled and snorted and danced in the spring showers, until it was time for dinner. Then farmer Potter filled their trough with slop, a pig's favorite dinner, and they ate and ate and ate.

Farmer Potter had four goats living on his farm as well. They were all from the same family. Sam was the big brother, Sadie was the big sister and Sugar and Cinder were their twin baby sisters.

Sam and Sadie loved their baby sisters and were always nice to them. They shared their hay, played hide and go seek in the tall weeds around their barnyard, and when it was cold they would all cuddle inside the goat shed to keep warm. Farmer Potter had sold their parents to another farmer, so they knew they had to stick together and look out for each other.

Yes, Sam and Sadie were always kind to Sugar and Cinder, but they were not always nice to the other animals.

Sadie climbed on top of the goat shed and watched the chickens and the pigs. She called out to her brother Sam, *"Baaaa! Look at those baby chickens! They don't even have feathers, yet Papa Rooster struts and crows like they are the cutest babies ever. Baaaa! They look like bald little runts to me."*

"Baaaa, ha ha!" Sam laughed with Sadie and pointed at the little chicks with his hoof. *"Those runts can't even cluck properly! Baaaa!"*

Mama Hen puffed up her feathers, *"Cluck, cluck"* and took her babies under her wings. She hurried them into the chicken coop so they wouldn't hear the teasing while Papa Rooster scolded the older goats.

"Cock-a-doodle-do! If you can't say anything nice, you shouldn't say anything at all!"

Sadie paid no attention to Papa Rooster. With the chickens huddled safe in their coop, Sadie started picking on Maisy and Daisy. *"Hey Piggies!" she called. "Do you know how Baaaa'd you smell? Pretty Baaaa'd!"*

Sam laughed at his sister's teasing, but Maisy and Daisy only grunted and tried to ignore her. Sadie kept bullying.

"Dirty piggies eat your slop. Eat, eat, eat, until you pop, pop, pop! Baaaa-ha-ha!"

Maisy and Daisy looked down at the mud. They didn't like it when Sadie was mean and bullied them, but there was nothing they could do. Sadie was pretty, and she could climb high and run fast. She had Sam, Sugar and Cinder on her side. Maisy and Daisy only had each other and their puddles, so they turned their curly tails to the goat shed and wallowed down in the cool wet mud.

One especially warm spring day, in the late afternoon while Sadie and Sam were grazing in their field, Farmer Potter pulled up to the barnyard in his truck. Attached to his truck was a horse trailer. The chickens and pigs peeked through the fence to see what was going on. Sam and Sadie ran to the goat shed to protect Sugar and Cinder from whatever might be in the trailer. Sadie snorted, *"Baaaa, I hope we aren't getting anymore chickens or pigs! We have enough of those!"*

Farmer Potter opened the trailer door and Sam heard him say, "There, there girl. You're okay. C'mon out and meet your new friends."

Sadie heard hooves clip-clopping down the trailer ramp. A large pair of furry ears popped up behind the trailer door, and the other animals stretched their necks to see what sort of beast would be attached to those ears. They were all startled and jumped when they heard a very loud *"HE-HAW, HE-HAW!"*

Two pretty brown eyes with long eyelashes peeked out from under those ears. The new girl looked around at all the other animals in the barnyard. The gentle eyes belonged to Esther.

Esther was a mini-donkey, a miniature Easter donkey to be exact. She noticed Maisy and Daisy first. The sister pigs smiled at the horse-like animal and happily squealed *"hello"* to Esther.

Esther flicked her ears back and forth to greet them, just as donkeys do. Esther saw the chickens next. She bent her head down to their coop as a sign of friendship, and they fluttered their feathers. *"Your babies are heee-haw precious!"* Esther gushed.

"Cluck, cluck, cluck!" Mama Hen thanked her.

Sadie watched the others welcome Esther, and thought how foolish they were to be so nice to a new animal they didn't even know.

"What is she anyhow?" Sadie hissed to Sam.

"If she's a horse, she's the ugliest one I ever saw," Sam answered.

Esther's extra-large ears heard everything, and she turned to face the goat herd. *"HEE-HAW!"* She brayed loudly. *"I'm a donkey, actually a miniature Easter donkey."* She stomped her front hoof on the ground to say hello.

"Ohhh, she's an Easter donkey! Baaaa!" Sadie teased. *"What does that even mean? Do you lay colorful eggs or carry a pretty basket? Are you full of jelly beans?"*

Sugar and Cinder snickered and giggled at big sister Sadie's cruel insults. *"Baa, baa, baa!"*

Maisy and Daisy snorted at Esther, *"Don't listen to them. Oink Oink. Sam and Sadie are bullies. We will be your friends. Oink!"*

Esther flicked her ears back and lowered her head as Farmer Potter led her to her own private shed in the barnyard. She could still hear the goats talking about her, but she didn't talk back.

She liked her new shed. There was fresh water to drink and warm straw for a bed. It would be dark soon and she was tired from her long trip to Potter's barnyard. She decided she would try to make friends with the goat family again in the morning.

As the sky got dark and the stars started to shine, all the critters large and small laid down to go to sleep. All of them, except Sugar and Cinder.

The two littlest goats waited for Sam and Sadie to go to sleep, then they crept quietly out of their shed. They were too curious about the new donkey to go to sleep. They wanted a closer look at Esther, so they climbed on top of their shed and jumped over the fence to Esther's pasture. Esther's big ears heard them and she opened one watchful eye.

As the little ones got closer to Esther's shed, she could hear them whispering.

"Easter has nothing to do with donkeys," Sugar was telling Cinder, *"it's all about bunnies and eggs."*

"Esther must have made up the idea of an 'Easter' donkey," Cinder replied.

Esther sighed sadly. *Nobody knows the true meaning of Easter anymore,* she thought. She decided she would tell Sugar and Cinder all about it once they got to her shed.

All of the sudden, a loud, scary, howling sound broke into the quiet night. Esther heard paws running fast through the long grass in her pasture and then the scared cries of Cinder and Sugar, *"Baaaa! Baaaaaa! Help!"*

The awful noise woke all the other animals, and they came out of their shelters to see what was happening. In the moonlight, all of the animals saw the same scary sight! Sugar and Cinder were backed up against Esther's shed, crying for help, while two very hungry coyotes circled and growled at them, licking their sharp teeth as they thought about eating the little goats.

Sadie and Sam gasped and cried out helplessly from the wrong side of the fence, *"Baa, Baa, Baa!"* Maisy and Daisy knelt in the mud and began to pray while the chickens stood frozen in fear.

Suddenly, a loud *"HEE-HAW, HEE-HAW"* came from Esther's shed and she charged out into the pasture. She ran right between the coyotes and the little goats, putting herself in danger to protect Sugar and Cinder.

The coyotes tried to jump on Esther and bite her legs, but she bucked wildly and kicked them away, *"HEE-HAW, HEE-HAW!"* The coyotes were vicious and Esther was scared, but she kept kicking and carrying on until the hungry beasts finally ran away.

When the scary fight was over, Esther guided the little goats into her shed and laid down beside them. The bite marks on her legs were painful, but she didn't complain. She quietly licked her wounds, and forgetting about Easter for the time being, she protected Sugar and Cinder inside her shed until the sun came up in the morning.

Farmer Potter found the little goats sharing Esther's shed in the morning and led them back to their own pen with Esther following close behind. When Farmer Potter was finished giving them all fresh water and food, the animals began to chat.

"You are a hero!" Maisy said. Daisy oinked loudly in agreement. The chickens cluck-clucked about how brave Esther had been and thanked her for saving Sugar and Cinder. Sadie was the only barnyard animal who was quiet. She just listened to the others with her head hung low. Esther noticed Sadie's silence and trotted over to the hay crib where Sadie stood.

When Sadie saw Esther standing in front of her, she couldn't be quiet any longer. She scratched the ground with her hoof and questioned Esther, *"Baa! Why? Why did you save my little sisters? You put your life in danger to save theirs. After we were so mean to you, why did you help us?"*

Esther stomped her hoof on the ground and took a bite of hay. Then she looked at Sadie and answered. *"Because, I am an Easter donkey. I was born to be forgiving and selfless, just like the real hero of the very first Easter was. Hee-Haw."*

"What do you mean?" Sadie asked. *"Are you talking about the Easter Bunny?"*

Esther snorted a friendly donkey giggle. *"Hee-Haw-Haw, No... I'm talking about Jesus. You do know who Jesus is, don't you?"*

By this time, all of the animals had gathered around to listen to Esther, and they all shook their heads, *"no."*

"Really?" Esther asked with her eyes wide. *"Well then, I must tell you about Jesus and my great-great-great-great grandmother Lilly, Hee-Haw."*

All the animals moved in close to Esther as she shared her story.

"Many years ago, the one true God who created the whole world and all of us animals and humans too, sent His son to earth as a baby. He was born in a stable like the ones we sleep in at night, and his name was Jesus."

Maisy and Daisy perked up their pink ears as they tried to imagine a tiny human sleeping in a stable, and Esther went on. *"His birthday is the day we call 'Christmas'. When Jesus grew up, he healed sick people and helped poor people. He and his friends taught people about God and love, everywhere they went. He said He was the perfect son of God, but some people didn't believe him. Those people were mean and picked on Jesus."*

Sadie interrupted Esther's story to ask, *"Were they mean to him like I was to you yesterday?"* Esther nodded her head up and down and then Sam asked, *"What did Jesus do?"*

Esther stomped the ground with her hoof again and twitched her tail back and forth. *"He asked God, his father, to forgive them. Then, since he knew that there would have to be a punishment for sin, Jesus took the punishment for everyone. He died, nailed to a cross, so all the people who hurt him could be saved and live forever in Heaven. He forgave them and protected them."*

Sadie didn't know what to say. She was amazed that Jesus would be so loving to all the people who hurt him. They didn't deserve his love and forgiveness, but he gave it to them anyway.

Finally, with a tear in her eye she said, *"That's incredible, but what does that have to do with you, or your great-great-great-great grandmother or what you did for Sugar and Cinder last night?"*

"Jesus died three days before Easter," Esther answered. *"My great-great-great-great grandmother, Lilly, was his donkey. She walked beside Jesus as he carried his cross all the way up the hill to where he was hung and died. She was so loyal, she never left his side. Do you see the two dark stripes on my back, the ones that form a cross on my shoulders?"*

Esther turned around so all the other animals could see her back and they all nodded when they saw the shape of a cross in her fur.

"Donkeys like me have a shadow of the cross on our backs as a reminder of the first Easter and in honor of grandmother Lilly's loyalty to Jesus as he suffered and died for all of mankind. Because I wear this mark of honor, it is my duty to love and protect others, even those who are not very nice to me, just as Jesus did."

The animals were quiet for a moment as Esther finished with her story. Finally Sadie spoke up.

"Baaa! That sounds like a very sad story. If that's what Easter is about, Jesus dying, why do we celebrate it?"

"Hee-haw," Esther answered, *"Because Easter is the day Jesus rose from the dead! Jesus died on the cross, but he didn't stay there. Three days later, God rose his son Jesus from the grave so he could live with his father in Heaven forever."* Esther's eyes twinkled, and she finished explaining.

"This was a miracle for everyone, because it meant that all of mankind would be able to go to heaven someday too, and live forever with God. Because Jesus took the punishment for everyone, anyone who asks for forgiveness will be forgiven and saved! That's why we celebrate Easter, and that's why I did what I could to save Sugar and Cinder when they were in danger."

Sadie and Sam both rose to their hind legs so they could give Esther a hug. With a tear in her eye, Sadie asked, *"Will you forgive me for being so awful to you when you arrived yesterday? I am very sorry."*

Esther nodded and brayed happily, *"HEE-HAW! Of course!"*

Then Sadie turned to all the others, Maisy, Daisy, Mother Hen and Papa Rooster. *"I am very sorry for being a bully to you all. Will you all forgive me? I want us all to be friends for Easter this year."*

The pigs splashed in their puddles and the chickens clucked in agreement. Together they exclaimed *"Yes, yes, yes! This Easter we will love and forgive. We will be like Jesus!"*

Sadie danced happily and bleated, *"Baa...Baa... thank you everyone and thank you Jesus! Happy Easter to us all!"*

The End

Glossary

Bleat – to make the sound that a sheep or goat makes

Bray – to make the loud sound that a donkey makes

Bully - someone who is habitually cruel to others who are weaker

Crept - moved slowly and quietly in order to not be noticed

Cruel - a word used to describe people who hurt others and do not feel sorry about it

Forgive - to stop feeling angry or blaming someone for something they did

Gentle – being and showing a kind and quiet nature

Pasture – a large area of land where animals feed on the grass

Runt – an unusually small person or animal

Scolded – to correct or criticize harshly

Slop – food waste (garbage) fed to pigs

Stable – a building or shed where animals are sheltered and fed

Trough – a long shallow container from which farm animals eat or drink

Wallow – to roll around in deep mud or water

Note from the Author

Bullying is never okay. In this story, Esther overcomes her bullies by being kind and forgiving, just as Jesus was. It is always good to be kind and forgiving, but sometimes it's not enough to stop a bully from bullying. If you are being treated badly over and over again by a bully, be sure to tell a grown-up who can help you. No one deserves to be bullied.

About the Author

Nora Ballew writes Christian fiction and poetry for all ages. She lives in rural Pennsylvania with her husband and a menagerie of beloved pets, including several goats and her own mini Easter donkey! She is the mother of three grown daughters and is also a loving grandmother.

Parents can learn more about Nora and her work by visiting or following her at:

http://www.noraballew.com

https://www.facebook.com/NoraBallewAuthor

http://www.twitter.com/noraballew

If you or your child enjoyed "Esther the Easter Donkey," please help others find it by leaving a review at http://www.amazon.com/

Lightning Source UK Ltd.
Milton Keynes UK
UKRC02n0015010518
321899UK00026B/784